Dirt Boy

Erik Jon Slangerup

ILLUSTRATED BY John Manders

Albert Whitman & Company

Morton Grove, Illinois

To Dalton, an inspiration to dirt boys
everywhere. — E. J. S.

For Marian, my baby sister. — J. M.

Slangerup, Erik Jon
Dirt Boy / by Erik Jon Slangerup; illustrated by John Manders.
p. cm.
Summary: To avoid taking a bath, Fister Farnello runs away from home
and is befriended by Dirt Man, a filthy giant who lives in the woods.
ISBN 0-8075-4424-8
[1. Cleanliness—Fiction. 2. Baths—Fiction. 3. Runaways—Fiction.
4. Giants—Fiction] I. Manders, John, ill. II. Title. PZ7.S628847 Di 2000
[E]—dc21 99-039124

The illustrations are rendered in watercolor and gouache; additionally, acrylic
paint, crackle medium, modeling paste, colored pencils, sponges, fingers, and
old toothbrushes were used to turn Fister into Dirt Boy.
The typeface is BeoSans.
The design is by Scott Piehl.

Fister Farnello loved dirt.

Every day, he rolled round and round in it, making delicious mud pies which he snacked on. The mud squished and squashed under his feet, tickling his toes and making him laugh until dirt sprayed out of his nose!

Late one afternoon, Fister Farnello slowly returned home from the furthermost corner of his backyard. His clean-and-mean mother was waiting.

"Into the tub at once!" she shouted, "you smelly-stinky-mucky-gritty-grimy-grubby-little-dirt-boy!"

"No! No! Pleeeaaase!" Fister cried and begged. But Fister's mother would hear none of it, wrestling off his clothes and plopping them on the floor.

WITHDRAWN

His dirty clothes cast big clouds of dust —ka-poof!— until nobody could see a thing.

That's when Fister made his escape!

He heard his mother calling **"Fister Farnello-o-o-o-o!"** but he didn't look back.

Fister ran and ran from everything clean until he found himself deep in the woods. He climbed to the top of a small hill and nestled into a soft, cozy little dip, where he fell fast asleep.

The next day, Fister awoke to a terrible r-r-rumbling and sh-sh-shaking. He thought it was an earthquake!

"WHO'S THERE?" boomed a bellowing voice.

Fister Farnello had fallen asleep in the bellybutton of a giant!

"I AM DIRT MAN," the giant continued, "AND I HAVEN'T TAKEN A BATH IN A THOUSAND YEARS!"

When Fister could finally get to his feet, he shouted, **"OH YEAH?
WELL, I AM DIRT BOY! AND I HAVEN'T TAKEN A BATH
IN ALMOST TWO DAYS!"**

The giant peered down and smiled, flashing his moldy green teeth.
The two instantly became friends.

Dirt Man and Dirt Boy passed the time playing dirt games in the woods.

(Dirt Man usually won.)

Night after night, Fister Farnello's mother waited for him to come home until she fell asleep with a soft z-z-z-z-z.
But deep in the woods…

Fister ran around as Dirt Boy.

His hair got tanglier and scragglier with each passing day. A bird made a nest on one side. A family of country mice moved in on the other side. The birds chirped all day and the mice squeaked all night.

Then, down by his feet, all of a sudden —**sproing!**—a big purple mushroom sprouted between his toes! Then another ⌐**pop!**—and another ⌐ **pop! pop!**

The birds and mice on his head started to complain: "Peee-yuuuu!" they cried. "Can't you do something?" But Dirt Boy couldn't do anything. He didn't even have a toothbrush. So every time he opened his mouth, out came a thick green cloud of stink. **Blaaaaaaahhhh!**

"Mmmm," sighed Dirt Man as he paused to lick the mildew off a rock. "You don't look so bad to me."

A patch of stray weeds curled and twisted out of Dirt Boy's nostrils. And a damp clump of moss started to creep out of his bellybutton. His skin felt so icky and slimy that he began to cry...big, muddy tears.

"Not to worry, my rotten little friend," said the giant. "You smell fine to me." He leaned over and took a couple of whiffs: **Squnorffk! Snorf!** "Mmmmmm…just like dirt…so ripe…so…" The giant sniffed again.

"So…**DELICIOUS!**"

Then Dirt Man the Giant greedily smacked his grimy lips, crouched way down, and sucked in as hard as he could with a terrible

MMMMMWWWWRRRRRAAAAAHHH!

The giant sucked in trees and boulders and rivers and clouds...

but not Dirt Boy.

Fister Farnello ran and ran back through the woods until he happened upon something familiar.

But Fister's mother took one look and screeched, "A monster!"
Fister tried to say, "Mom, it's me," but his teeth were so covered with gunk, all that came out was **"Mmmrrarrgh oorff pplllptt!"**
"Shoo! Shoo!" shouted his mother. She flapped her broom at him and tried to drive him back into the woods.

When that didn't work, she sprayed the monster with a hose.
Then an amazing thing happened. The water washed away some
of the dirt, leaving the faint shape of a certain long-lost boy. Fister's
mother paused. *Could it be?* She stepped a little closer.

"Fister, is that you?" she whispered hopefully. Fister used the dirt from his fingers to spell out…

It took twenty-three bars of soap, sixteen bottles of shampoo, one hundred and seventy-nine gallons of bathwater, forty-four million bubbles, and eleven tubes of toothpaste to finally get Fister Farnello clean. Ahhhhh, something was different, Fister thought to himself.

His skin felt soft and smooth. His breath was fresh, and his face was shiny and bright. And when at last he finished his bath, Fister felt lighter, as if walking on air. He floated into his mother's arms and gently drifted off to sleep.

Word of young Fister's wild adventures traveled quickly. His name became known throughout the neighborhood and across the land.

For a long time, Fister and his mother kept watch for Dirt Man the Giant out in the woods, but he was never seen or heard from again. Today, Fister Farnello still likes to get dirty...

...but he also likes to get clean.